Ned Breaks His Heart

by David Michael Slater

illustrated by S.G. Brooks

visit us at www.abdopublishing.com

For Hailey—DMS

Published by Magic Wagon, a division of the ABDO Group, 8000 West 78th Street, Edina, Minnesota 55439. Copyright © 2010 by Abdo Consulting Group, Inc. International copyrights reserved in all countries. All rights reserved. No part of this book may be reproduced in any form without written permission from the publisher.

Looking Glass Library™ is a trademark and logo of Magic Wagon.

Printed in the United States.

 Manufactured with paper containing at least 10% post-consumer waste

Text by David Michael Slater
Illustrations by S.G. Brooks
Edited by Stephanie Hedlund and Rochelle Baltzer
Interior layout and design by Becky Daum
Cover design by Becky Daum

Library of Congress Cataloging-in-Publication Data
Slater, David Michael.
  Ned breaks his heart / by David Michael Slater ; illustrated by S.G. Brooks.
    p. cm.
  Summary: Ned is heartsick when his model of a human heart is damaged in school, but he tries wholeheartedly to save it.
  ISBN 978-1-60270-657-6 (alk. paper)
  [1. Heart—Fiction. 2. Models and modelmaking—Fiction. 3. English language—Idioms—Fiction.]
I. Brooks, S. G., ill. II. Title.
  PZ7.S62898Nc 2009
  [E]—dc22
                          2008055340

"NED!" cried Mrs. Chambers. "Watch out!"

Ned looked up, and his heart nearly stopped. He couldn't even manage a halfhearted attempt to get out of the way.

The last thing Ned heard before everything went black was,

"OH NO!
MY HEART GOES OUT TO THAT POOR BOY!"

Ned sat up and looked around for his science project.
It was gone! This was heartbreaking! He'd worked
really hard on that model heart. He had his heart set on
winning a prize!

Still a little dizzy, Ned got to his feet. That's when he
spotted the model in the next display! His heart skipped
a beat as he stumbled toward it.

Ned had to know if his model heart was broken.

It wasn't! But . . .

. . . his real heart was!

Deep down, Ned knew he could mend his broken heart. After all, he'd built one with his own two hands! But how do you fix something that's inside you? Ned began to worry.

Finally, he started to cry . . .

Ned cried and cried. First his heart was in his throat . . . then it was in his mouth . . . then on his sleeve. Then his heart was in his hands! **He'd cried his heart out!**

Now Ned could use the model to fix his broken heart! It was time to get to the heart of the matter.

Ned was a hard worker. He poured his heart into cutting, screwing, zipping, and stitching.

Finally, he was done. That's when the kid at the next table, Hartley, pointed at his tower and said,

"Eat your heart out, Ned!"

Ned knew his heart deserved a ribbon. He just needed to get his heart back in his chest where it belonged. He had a plan, but he wasn't sure he was strong enough to go through with it. He hardened his heart . . .

INTERR

The followin
for the fa

UPTION:

scene is not
t of heart

Suddenly Ned's heart was in his throat again . . .

Soon enough,

it was back in his chest where it belonged.

With his heart in the right place,

Ned opened his eyes.

"NED!"

cried Mrs. Chambers.

"Are you okay? I nearly had a heart attack!"

"Don't worry, Mrs. Chambers," Ned said.
"I'm a hearty person."

"But your project! It's ruined! My heart bleeds for you, Ned!

I'm so sorry, from the bottom of my heart!"

"Take heart, Mrs. Chambers," Ned replied. "I have a great idea. **Cross my heart.**"

Idioms in *Ned Breaks His Heart*

An idiom is an expression that means something different than the words would by themselves. Here are the meanings for some of the idioms in this book:

Eat your heart out—I can do this better than you

Had his heart set on—decided to do something

Halfhearted attempt—trying without interest or excitement

Heart goes out to—feels sympathy for someone

Heart skipped a beat—suddenly surprised or excited

About the Author

David Michael Slater lives and teaches seventh grade Language Arts in Portland, Oregon. He uses his talents to educate and entertain with his humorous books and informative presentations. David writes for children, young adults, and adults. Some of his other titles include *Cheese Louise*, *The Ring Bear* (an SSLI-Honor Book), and *Jacques & Spock* (a Children's Book-of-the-Month Alternate Selection). More information about David and his books can be found at **www.abdopublishing.com**.